# Contents

# JENNY OLDFIELD

# Bright Star

With illustrations by
**Gary Blythe**

For Lola, Jude and Evan
– three bright stars in my sky

First published in 2014 in Great Britain by
Barrington Stoke Ltd
18 Walker Street, Edinburgh, EH3 7LP

www.barringtonstoke.co.uk

Text © 2014 Jenny Oldfield
Illustrations © 2014 Gary Blythe

A CIP catalogue record for this book is available
from the British Library upon request

ISBN: 978-1-78112-375-1

Printed in China by Leo

# Chapter 1
# City Girl

Morgan sat in the car and waited for her mom.

She looked up at the apartment on the 12th floor where she'd lived for 13 years.

Those 13 years were all of Morgan's life so far – a life of listening to her mom and dad fight like cat and dog, of watching daytime TV and of standing on the tiny balcony to hear the rattle and roll of trains 12 floors below.

Morgan held her bag on her lap.  She watched the wind blow litter across the parking lot – a blue plastic bag, an empty beer can.

At last Morgan's mom showed up. Her name was Lacey and that's what she liked Morgan to call her.

"OK, let's go," Lacey said.

Lacey drove Morgan along the early morning streets between the tower blocks. Soon they were out of Chicago and heading to O'Hare airport.

"Did you say goodbye to Gayla?" Lacey asked.

"Nope," Morgan mumbled.

"Brooke?" Lacey asked.

"Nope."

Lacey rolled her eyes. "Didn't you tell any of your friends you were leaving?"

"No, I didn't," Morgan said. "What would be the point?" She stared out of the window.

There was silence until they came to the airport.

"You got everything you need?" Lacey asked, when they had parked.

"Yep," Morgan said.

"Your phone?"

"Yep."

"Aunt Anne Marie's number?"

"Yep."

"Call me as soon as you land," Lacey said. "And give me a smile, why don't you?"

Morgan sighed. She was leaving the city for who knew how long, to live in some god-awful ranch in the Rocky Mountains with her aunt, Anne Marie. What was there to smile about?

Lacey came with Morgan to the check-in desk. "Hug?" she asked.

Morgan hugged her. Then she showed her ticket to the woman behind the American Airlines desk.

"Bye!" Lacey called as Morgan headed for her Departure Gate.

All of a sudden, Morgan felt scared. She turned and waved, hoping her mom would still be there.

Her mom waved back.

Morgan waved again. Then she turned and walked on down a long, shiny walkway past long lines of passengers waiting to board their planes. She was alone and on her way.

★ ★ ★

In the plane at 30,000 feet, clouds spread below Morgan like a fluffy cream blanket.

The cabin crew served peanuts and Diet Coke. The fat guy in the seat next to her snoozed and snored.

At last, the Fasten Seatbelts sign came on.

"We'll have you on the ground in Denver in around ten minutes," the pilot informed them as the plane began to dip down past the clouds. Morgan felt a bump when the plane hit the ground, then she heard the sharp whine of brakes. Out of the window, she could see mountains in the distance. It was late June, but the peaks were still white with snow.

* * *

A tall guy in a dusty cowboy hat stepped forward to greet Morgan at Baggage Reclaim.

"Anne Marie couldn't make it," he said. "Sunday means new guests arrive at the ranch. She's busy, so she sent me instead.  I'm Ryan. Hi."

A cowboy hat! No kidding – he was wearing a real live Stetson and cowboy boots. Morgan had only ever seen them on TV. When she shook his hand, it felt rough.

"Morgan," she said. She felt herself blush bright red.

"Let's go." Ryan took Morgan's bag and led her to an old Ford truck. He waited for Morgan to climb into the front, then they set off for the ranch. Along the way, Ryan played country and western music, stopped for gas, and bought Morgan a bag of spicy corn chips and a bottle of water.

After an hour and a half, the road rose out of the flat Denver plains up into the mountains. "We're halfway there," Ryan told her.

Morgan saw a dead deer by the side of the road, a few trailer homes just off the highway, and miles of pine forest. The highway was empty except for huge, rumbling trucks and the odd car now and then.

After three long hours, Ryan turned left onto a dirt track. They drove under a rough wooden arch. There was a sign showing a row of three horseshoes. The ends pointed up.

"Welcome to Three Horseshoes Ranch," Ryan said.

* * *

Morgan's Aunt Anne Marie was carrying a horse's saddle across a crowded horse pen.

"Did you call your mom?" she yelled at Morgan when she spotted her on the porch of the ranch house.

"Yeah!" Morgan yelled back.

"Cool," Anne Marie said. "Go into the kitchen, grab a cheese sandwich."

There was no "Hi, how are you?" No guided tour of the ranch. Morgan's aunt was far too busy with her new guests all afternoon and evening.

"See those boots?" Anne Marie asked a while later.  She had swung by the porch with a sack of grain pellets.  "The ones by the door?"

Morgan saw a pair of battered cowboy boots and nodded.

"My old ones – try them on," her aunt told her.

"What?"

"Take off your sneakers and try on the boots.  See if they fit."

"They fit," Morgan said.  It was true, but the pointed toes squeezed her feet.

"Cool," said Anne Marie.  "After you finish your sandwich, I could use some help with the horses."

Cowboy boots, Stetsons, heavy saddles, grain pellets, plus 20 horses lined up outside ...

It was too much for Morgan to take in. And the smells! She breathed in wild flowers from the meadow, sweat and pee from the horses, coffee from the kitchen.

"Quit just standing there like a city girl, Morgan," Anne Marie yelled as she disappeared into the barn. "Ask Ryan – he'll tell you what to do!"

## Chapter 2
# Three Horseshoes

"So your mom and dad split up at last?" Anne Marie asked at supper that night.

Morgan pushed food around her plate. She didn't answer the question.

"And you skipped school for how long?"

Silence again from Morgan. She hadn't gone to school for five whole weeks. She'd spent the time hanging out in the shopping mall or at the park instead. What was the point of going to classes? What was the point of anything when your dad had left home and didn't answer your calls?

"OK, I get it," Anne Marie said. "You don't want to discuss it. So, anyway, Lacey reckons a change of scene will do you good. How do you like ranch life so far?"

'Dusty, dirty, smelly, lonely, scary …' The words piled up into a log-jam inside Morgan's head.

Anne Marie grinned. "Not what a city girl is used to – huh?" she said. She got up from the table and stacked dishes into the dishwasher. "So how do you feel about working with horses?"

'Dusty, dirty, smelly …'

Anne Marie closed the dishwasher and studied Morgan's sulky face. "Don't say much, do you?"

"Nope."

"Hmm," Anne Marie said. "At least you and Ryan will get along."

"How come?"

"He doesn't say much either – just works, eats and sleeps."

"Fine by me," Morgan mumbled as she stomped upstairs to bed.

* * *

That night, what got to Morgan was the silence. And the stars.

There were a million stars, tiny and twinkling. And the silence was so complete it got inside her head and cleared out all the muck that was in there.

Morgan went to sleep still gazing out at the stars. When she woke the stars were gone, but the silence was still with her.

She got out of bed and looked out of the window at the sun rising over mountains to the east. There was a low mist in the valley. A group of deer was feeding on a rocky slope, and there were horses in the meadow.

Morgan heard a tiny sound that turned out to be the click of a gate as Ryan strode out to fetch the horses into the pen.

'Lonely, scary ...' The old words started to fade and new ones floated in.

'Peaceful, beautiful, amazing ...'

★ ★ ★

When Morgan went downstairs and smelled bacon, she knew she was hungry.

She ate the bacon with scrambled eggs and two slices of wholemeal toast. Then Anne Marie took her out to the horse pen.

"What do I do with this?" Morgan asked when her aunt handed her a big plastic shovel.

Anne Marie pointed to the heaps of horse dung lying in the dirt. "You scoop the poop and toss it in the trailer."

Morgan pulled a face. "Disgusting! No way! Not in a million years!"

Ryan smiled. "Like this," he said, showing her how. He slid between the horses, scooped the dung and tossed it in the trailer. "Don't get behind the horses," he warned. "They kick. And hard."

'Somebody tell me this isn't happening,' Morgan thought. 'I can't do this! I want to go home!'

⋆ ⋆ ⋆

At ten that morning, the ranch guests came down from their cabins ready to ride. There was a family from Texas – mom, dad, two kids – plus two couples from Florida and a group of women riders from California.

Morgan watched Ryan and Anne Marie hold the horses' reins as the guests climbed into the saddle. The guys from Florida acted like they knew everything. One of the Texan kids cried and said she didn't want to get on her horse. At long last they were ready, and Anne Marie mounted her horse and led them out on the trails.

"More scooping," Ryan said as he handed Morgan the shovel again. "And try not to step in any puddles of pee."

It turned out that Ryan was 18 years old. He lived in Whitewater, which was the nearest town, 15 miles down the road.

For a guy who didn't say much, he gave Morgan plenty of information.

"I finished school last summer but I knew college wasn't my thing," he told her. "I like horses better than people, so in January I came to work for Anne Marie."

"I hate horses," Morgan told him. A morning's work with the shovel was enough to tell her this.

"Huh."

"They kick and bite and they throw you off," she said. "Plus, they look at you in a weird way."

"What kind of weird?" Ryan asked.

"They roll their eyes like they're mad at you."

"Yeah." Ryan didn't look convinced.

"I hate them," Morgan said again.

Ryan said nothing, just nodded and handed her a rake.

"What do I do with this?" Morgan asked.

★ ★ ★

After a day of scooping and raking, lifting and carrying, Morgan watched Ryan get in his truck to drive home from Three Horseshoes.

Anne Marie invited Morgan to eat supper with the guests, but she said "no thanks". She stayed in the kitchen and ate alone instead. She went to bed soon after the sun had set, and she woke at dawn.

Out in the yard, Morgan found Ryan loading wooden posts and razor wire into the back of his truck.

"You want to come?" he asked.

"Where to?"

"Wildflower Lake," he said. "I need to fix the fence."

"OK," Morgan said. She thought it would be better to fix a fence than scoop poop at any rate.

So they rode out along a different dirt track, through the pine forest until they came to a lake.

"Wow!  It's big!" Morgan said.

The water went on and on.  The bright feathers of a Blue Jay caught the sunlight as the bird flew up from the long grass into a nearby tree.  The blue of the sky matched the vast blue of the lake, and the mountain peaks beyond were tipped with white.

"Here, catch!"  Ryan took a battered straw hat from his cab and threw it at Morgan. "Wear that," he said.

She caught it.  "Why?"

"For the sun, stupid."

Morgan scowled but she jammed the old hat down on her head.  She watched Ryan hammer a post into the ground, then she put on some thick gloves and handed him a coil of razor wire.

They worked together in silence. Then, before Morgan knew it, the sun was high in the sky, there was sweat on her head under the hat and she had to take a break.

Morgan sat on a rock, drank some water and looked out across the lake.

Ryan sat down beside her. "See that?" he asked. He pointed to the water's edge.

"No – what?" Morgan looked hard and at last she saw what he was pointing at.

About 50 paces from where they sat, there was a boulder and some bushes, and hidden there was a black horse with a tangled mane. It was skinny and dusty, like nobody cared for it. The horse lowered its head to drink, raised it again, then stared right at them.

"Her name's Bright Star," Ryan said.

The horse went on staring as Morgan watched her. She was pure black except for a white star on her forehead.

"Wait here," Ryan told Morgan.

He took a rope from the truck and in four swift movements he tied it into a loop. Then he stepped through a break in the razor wire of the fence and walked slowly towards the horse.

Bright Star watched him. She pricked her ears and swished her tail. When Ryan raised his arm to throw the rope, she exploded into action.

Up in the air on her back legs, ragged mane flying, hooves pawing the air. Then down and turning, breaking into a gallop, fleeing the rope.

The rope splashed into the lake. Bright Star was gone.

# Chapter 3
# Wild Mustang

Morgan and Ryan worked on the fence until late afternoon.  Now they were in the truck on their way back to the ranch.

"How come you know her name?" Morgan asked.

"Whose name?" said Ryan.

"Bright Star's."  Morgan couldn't get the picture of the skinny, dusty horse by the lake out of her head.

"Because she's Anne Marie's horse," Ryan said.

"So why isn't she in the meadow with the others?"

"Because," Ryan said.  Then he shook his head.

"Because ... what?"  Morgan remembered how the black horse had reared, how her mane flew back, how she galloped away.

"Because she's wild, that's why," Ryan told her.  "A wild mustang.  The government brought her in from a herd in the desert in California.  Your aunt adopted her and named her Bright Star.  She wanted to tame her."

"But Bright Star didn't want to be tamed?" Morgan said.  She looked up over the trees towards a high, rocky ridge.  She scanned the horizon, hoping to see the wild horse again.

"Nope," Ryan said.  "That horse loves her freedom."

"So she escaped?" Morgan asked.

Ryan smiled. "Jumped clean over the fence in the meadow – there wasn't a thing we could do to stop her."

"Wow!" Morgan sighed. "But she'll be OK – out there, all alone?"

Ryan drove on without answering.

"She will, won't she?" Morgan asked him again.

"Until winter comes," he told her.

"Then what?"

"Then we get snow. A horse has nothing to eat when the ground is covered in snow."

"And that means she dies?"

Ryan nodded. "Either she freezes to death or she starves – end of story."

★   ★   ★

"We saw Bright Star out by Wildflower Lake," Morgan told Anne Marie when they got back. She'd found her in the tack room, hanging up bridles.

Anne Marie shook her head and sighed. "That horse!"

"She's so skinny," Morgan said.

"Yep."

"She looked scared."

"That's because wild horses like to be in a herd," Anne Marie told her. "That way they feel safe."

"So why won't she come back and join the others?" Morgan asked.

Anne Marie stopped what she was doing. She frowned and sighed again. "The truth is

Bright Star doesn't trust us," she told Morgan. "At least, she doesn't trust me.  That's why she ran away."

★ ★ ★

Later, Morgan went for a walk by the creek. Dusk was falling.  As the sky darkened, the first bright star appeared above her.

Bright Star!  Morgan couldn't stop thinking about the wild horse.  She looked for her among the pine trees and on the rocky ridges.  She listened for the sound of her hooves.

But all she heard was Ryan calling, "See you tomorrow!", as he rattled along the track on his way home.

The noise of Ryan's truck startled a group of mule deer, which bounded up the slope into the trees.

Morgan watched them run.  Then she raised her gaze to the high ridge above the meadow.

There she was – Bright Star.  She stood still as a statue on the horizon, and stared down at Morgan.

'It can't be true,' Morgan thought. 'I must be imagining it.' She blinked, then looked again.

Bright Star was still there – high up on the ridge. The sky behind her was a deep violet blue. The horse didn't move.

Morgan pictured the same scene in December – a metre of snow on the ground, cold wind gusting through the pine trees. She knew that winter would be long and hard out here in the Rockies.

"Either she freezes to death or she starves," Ryan had warned.

Morgan felt a shiver of fear for the wild horse. "Come back, Bright Star!" she whispered. "Come back to the ranch."

"That horse loves her freedom," Ryan had said.

And there she was now – up on the ridge, a clear black shape against the violet sky, watching Morgan.  Alone and free.

# Chapter 4
## Caspar

On Wednesday morning, Lacey called from Chicago.

"Hi honey, how are you?" she asked. "Is Anne Marie OK? How do you like ranch life?"

The usual chit-chat.

"Good. She's fine. It's OK," Morgan said.

Her mom didn't have much news, so the call was brief.

"Love you, honey.  Miss you!" Lacey said as she rang off.

* * *

"So, today you learn how to ride," Anne Marie told Morgan.  "It's time."

"Me?"  Morgan didn't want to do any such thing.  She picked up a spade and began to scoop poop.

"Sure," Anne Marie said.  "Ryan's brought Caspar in from the meadow for you.  Caspar, meet Morgan.  Morgan, this is Caspar."

Caspar was not a pretty horse – even Morgan realised that.  His coat was grey with flecks of black.  He had a stringy black mane and hardly any tail.

"He may not be much to look at, but he has a big heart," Anne Marie said, as if she could read Morgan's mind.

"You want me to ride him?" Morgan asked. This was crazy. Didn't her aunt know how much Morgan hated horses?

"Step up," Anne Marie said.

Morgan realised that she had no choice. She put her left foot in the stirrup and swung her right leg over Caspar's back. Whoa, this felt high off the ground!

"Now grab the reins," Anne Marie told her.

Morgan took a deep breath, then did as she was told.

"Squeeze with both legs," Anne Marie instructed. "There you go!"

Caspar began to walk around the horse pen. Morgan swayed and slipped in the saddle until at last she got her balance.

"Give him a little kick," Anne Marie said as she watched her.

'OK then,' Morgan thought. Kick.

Caspar broke into a trot. Morgan jiggled in the saddle. Up-down, up-down. Talk about scary!

"OK, pull on the reins," Anne Marie said. "Gentle, now."

Morgan pulled.  Caspar stopped.  Morgan was amazed.

"Cool," Anne Marie said.  "For a city girl who's never been on a horse before, you did good."

★  ★  ★

On Wednesday night, Morgan helped her aunt cook steak on the barbecue out on the back lawn.  For the first time, she ate with the guests.

On Thursday, she rode Caspar again and Ryan taught her how to lope.

"Sit deep in the saddle, relax – there you go!" he told her.

Caspar loped along the trail, good as gold. Then Morgan turned the horse and walked him back to the pen, took off his saddle and led him to the water barrels.  She stood back as Caspar began to drink.

"You like him?" Ryan asked.

"He's OK," Morgan muttered.

But she patted Caspar behind Ryan's back and gave him an apple as a treat.  She smiled when she heard the horse's big teeth crunch the fruit.

"More than OK," Morgan said to herself. She patted Caspar's gentle grey neck and stroked his soft nose.

On Friday, Morgan rode out with the two Texan kids.  She and Caspar led the ride across the meadow and up onto the ridge where she'd last seen Bright Star.  She looked for the runaway black horse, but no – she was nowhere to be seen.

"Good job," Ryan told her when Morgan brought the guests back.

'I did it!' Morgan thought. 'And it turns out I don't hate horses after all. How cool is that!'

★ ★ ★

"Why does the lid of the grain barrel have a lock on it?" Morgan asked Ryan.

It was Saturday morning and they were busy mucking out the horses together.

"To keep out the bears," he said.

"Bears come into the barn?" Morgan gasped.

Ryan nodded.

"Do bears attack horses?" she asked.

"Nope," Ryan said. "But mountain lions do. They'd hunt and attack a lone horse."

"Do we have mountain lions around here?"

"We sure do."

Morgan was kept busy all day, but that night she dreamed about a mountain lion creeping up on Bright Star. The big cat's yellow eyes glinted as it jumped on the horse's back and sank its sharp teeth into her flesh. In her dream, Morgan was helpless to stop it. She woke up with a start, got out of bed and stood at the window. She looked out at the moonlit ridge, hoping to see the runaway horse.

"Please come back, Bright Star!" she whispered into the emptiness.

★ ★ ★

Morgan woke at sunrise next morning and made a big decision. "I can't leave Bright Star out there!" she said to herself. "I just can't."

She got out of bed, went down and brought Caspar in from the meadow.

"You're up early," Anne Marie called from the porch of the ranch house.

"I need to find Bright Star," Morgan told her.

Her aunt jogged over to join her in the horse pen. "Then what?" she asked.

"Then I'll feed her treats and she'll know I'm her friend," Morgan said. She patted her saddle bag. "She'll learn to trust me and then she'll let me bring her home."

"Good luck with that," Anne Marie said.

Morgan could tell by her aunt's voice that she didn't think Morgan's plan would work. But Morgan was determined. She squeezed Caspar's sides and steered him out the gate. They walked along the misty valley, up into the forest.

"We're looking for Bright Star," Morgan told Caspar. "I need you to help me."

Caspar seemed to understand. He threw back his head and let out a loud neigh.

Together, Morgan and Caspar listened hard – but there was no answering call.

They walked on past the tall pine trees to the ridge above the ranch. Caspar neighed again. This time Morgan heard a faint reply – a second horse neighing back.

Morgan's heart beat faster. "Again!" she told Caspar. Caspar neighed, and at the sound a horse appeared on the ridge.

Yes – it was Bright Star!

Caspar stopped. The wild mustang stopped too.

Morgan reached into her saddle bag and pulled out an apple. She nudged Caspar's flanks and the horse moved slowly forward. Bright Star watched. She flicked her ears, swished her tail. Waiting, waiting ...

When they were ten metres from Bright Star, Morgan held out the apple.

Just then, Ryan's truck rattled along the track in the valley below.  The noise broke the stillness.

Bright Star was spooked.  She reared up and whirled away from Caspar and Morgan.

Morgan sat and watched her gallop off.

# Chapter 5
# The Search

Morgan didn't give in.

Every chance she got, she rode out on Caspar to look for Bright Star. They went up onto the ridge then down into the valley beyond, where Wildflower Lake sparkled in the sun.

"Nothing?" Anne Marie asked Morgan when she got back to the ranch on the Monday morning.

"No sign," Morgan said.

Morgan gave Caspar an apple for a treat, then brushed the dirt out of his grey coat. She used a wide-tooth comb to get the tangles out of his black mane.

"See anything?" Ryan asked on the Tuesday.

"Nothing," Morgan said.

"How far did you go?" he asked.

"Almost to the lake this time," Morgan told him. "It was getting dark, so we had to turn back."

"The lake is a good place to look," Ryan said.

"Yeah. I'll try again – maybe early tomorrow morning."

★ ★ ★

"Hey, honey." It was Morgan's mom on the phone again. The call came on Wednesday,

before Morgan and Caspar set off for
Wildflower Lake. "You settling in OK?" Lacey
asked.

"Yeah, it's cool," Morgan said. "I like it
here."

There was a pause, then Lacey tried to
sound cheerful. "Cool," she said. "That's good.
I'm glad it's working out. No, really – hey, gotta
go – bye!"

"Bye," Morgan said. She'd wanted to talk
more, but her mom had ended the call.

Morgan texted Lacey after she'd tipped
bales of hay into a metal feeder, then scooped
poop with Anne Marie. "I miss you," she wrote.
She put a row of three hearts after the words
and then sent the message to her mom.

★   ★   ★

The sun was high in the sky, so Morgan pulled the brim of her hat low over her forehead. 'Jeez, it's hot!' she thought. She looked down at the lake. "Do you see anything?" she asked Caspar.

Caspar looked and listened. He threw back his head and neighed.

Silence – so much of it, so deep and still. Morgan sighed. Caspar walked on.

At last they reached the lake. Morgan knew that Caspar would be thirsty, and so she slipped down from the saddle, loosened the strap round his middle and led him to the water. She waited while the horse drank.

Then she heard something move – a deer perhaps? The sound came from the area where Morgan and Ryan had fixed the fence, about 50 paces from the water's edge. Caspar stopped drinking, raised his head and listened. He'd heard it, too.

Caspar flicked his ears in the direction of the sound.

"What is it?" Morgan whispered.

Caspar neighed softly. Then they both heard a horse neigh back at them.

"It's Bright Star – we've found her at last!" Morgan cried. Her heart soared. Sure as anything, the wild horse was over there between the pine trees, by the wire fence.

"Treat!" Morgan said to herself. "Take her a treat."

She reached into her saddle bag, got out an apple and then walked with Caspar over to the fence. "Bright Star will eat the apple," Morgan told Caspar. "I'll be her buddy and she'll trust me to take her home!"

All of a sudden, Caspar stopped in the long grass growing by the edge of the lake. It came up to his knees. "OK, you wait here," Morgan told him, surprised. She strode on alone until she came to a section of wire fence hidden by bushes. "OK, I get it," she muttered. "You don't like the look of the razor wire."

Morgan had to stoop low and crawl under the wire. "Call again!" she told Caspar and Caspar neighed.

Morgan heard Bright Star's neigh in reply. She changed direction and followed the sound. "Hey, there you are!" she murmured when at last she saw the black horse.

Bright Star stood in the long grass on the far side of the fence. She didn't move away from Morgan, but her ears were flat against her head and she looked scared.

'At least this time she's not running away,' Morgan thought. She drew closer.

She could see that Bright Star's neck and chest were wet with sweat. Her eyes rolled and Morgan smelled hot fear. She knew there must be a reason why the wild horse didn't run – and when she looked more closely she saw what it was.

Bright Star was trapped.

A loose coil of sharp razor wire lay hidden in the grass, attached to one of the posts. Bright Star had stepped right onto it. The wire had snared her back leg and had cut her flesh when she'd tried to pull free. Morgan could see that the harder Bright Star had pulled, the more cruelly the wire had bitten her.

Morgan gasped. She had never seen such pain and fear. She felt sick to her stomach.

'It's my fault,' she thought. 'I must have left the wire there by mistake. Now Bright Star is trapped. If I don't help her, she could bleed to death!'

# Chapter 6
## Lucky Stars

"What do I do?"

"I can't leave her here to die!"

Questions flashed through Morgan's mind as she stared at the deep cuts on Bright Star's leg.

Caspar rustled his way through the long grass and stopped at the fence.

Bright Star breathed hard and rolled her eyes.

"Please don't be scared!" Morgan whispered. "We're here to help."

It was easy to say the words, but Morgan's heart was thumping and she had no idea what came next. Even if Bright Star would let her get close enough to untangle her, the sharp blades of the wire would cut Morgan's hands to shreds.

'Gloves!' she thought. 'I need gloves.'

Morgan crawled back under the wire fence, then ran to Caspar, opened the saddle bag and pulled out the thick work gloves she'd used the last time she was here. She pulled them on and went back.

"Easy, now," she murmured to Bright Star. "Stand still – good girl, nice and easy!"

But the poor horse was shaking and sweating, and her body pulsed with fear.

"Easy, easy!" Morgan said over and over, as gently as she could. She winced at the sight of dark red blood pouring from the cuts down Bright Star's leg, but she knew she had to be brave. "Trust me!" she whispered as she crouched and took hold of the wire. "I'm sorry if this hurts."

The wire was strong. It took Morgan ages to unwind it from around Bright Star's leg.

"Don't move until I'm done," she pleaded. "Easy, now."

As Morgan untangled the wire from Bright Star's leg, she thought of how the horse must be feeling. Bright Star was wild. She didn't trust people because people had taken her away from her beautiful desert home. She wanted to kick and rear and run. But if she did, the wire would cut even deeper into her leg and she would die. So Bright Star stood in fear while Morgan worked.

Inch by inch, Morgan unwound the wire.

Morgan felt Bright Star tremble as she worked. But then she felt the horse's pain ease and she lowered her head closer to Morgan. Morgan looked up. She took off her glove and reached to stroke the white star on the horse's head.

Bright Star's warm breath fell across Morgan's cheek. Morgan sensed the words "Thank you!" in her breath.

"Wait here," Morgan murmured. She went back under the fence and returned with Caspar's lead rope and head collar. "Here, let me put this on you," she said to Bright Star. "You trust me now, don't you? You're gonna wait here with us – me and Caspar. I'll take out my phone and call Three Horseshoes. They'll drive the trailer out to fetch us. Is that OK?"

The sound of Morgan's voice seemed to soothe Bright Star. The horse stood still while Morgan bound her bleeding wounds with strips she'd torn from the bottom of her old, frayed shirt.

"Good girl," Morgan murmured. "Nice and easy. You and me, we're doing just fine."

★   ★   ★

Anne Marie and Ryan came out to the lake together. First they loaded Caspar onto the trailer, then they coaxed Bright Star in after him. They made space for Morgan in the cab and drove home.

"It was my fault," Morgan said, when Anne Marie unloaded Bright Star in the horse pen and inspected the cuts on her leg. "It was me – I left the razor wire lying on the ground."

"Nope," Ryan said. "It wasn't you." He went to the cab and lifted out the coil of wire that had trapped Bright Star. "See this?" he said. "It's rusted to hell."

"So? What difference does that make?" Morgan asked.

"This razor wire has been lying there, rusting away for months, maybe years," Ryan told her. "Someone dumped it there long before you got here."

"You think?" Morgan asked. She took a deep breath and felt a weight slide from her shoulders. She was so happy that none of this was her fault.

"I know," Ryan insisted. "And that horse has to thank her lucky stars that you and Caspar went looking for her. Without you, she'd be dead."

# Chapter 7
## You and Me Both

"I found Bright Star! I saved her life!" Morgan
was on the phone to her mom again. Words
tumbled out and ran together. "Bright Star
was wild, she didn't trust anyone, but she let
me and Caspar come near. And I worked at the
razor wire to free her. And she wasn't scared
of me cos she knew I was trying to help. And
we got her back to Three Horseshoes and Anne
Marie put her in a stall in the barn and she got
the vet to come and take a look. And the vet
says Bright Star will be fine, so everything's
cool and ..."

"Whoa – good job, Morgan!" Lacey laughed. "Listen, guess what I'm holding in my hand right now?"

"I don't know – tell me."

"A plane ticket to Denver."

"How come?" Morgan asked.

"It's for me," Lacey said. "I'm flying out to the ranch ... Morgan, are you still there?"

"Yeah, I'm here."

"I took time off work. I'm coming to visit," her mom said. "How cool is that?"

"When?"

"Next week. Morgan, speak to me – are you OK with this?"

"I guess," Morgan said.

"But ...?"

Morgan thought for a while. Yeah, she was cool with her mom being here at the ranch. Lacey could learn how to scoop poop and fill the metal feeders with hay. Who knew, she might even get to meet Bright Star.

"Better bring some boots," she told her. "And a hat for the sun, oh and a rain jacket and some old gloves – you'll need all of the above. And no fancy clothes, Lacey – you won't be wanting them."

★ ★ ★

Morgan sat on the stall door and watched Bright Star eat grain pellets from a wooden manger.

The vet had stitched Bright Star's wounds and bound them with a white bandage. He'd given her antibiotics and said for Anne Marie to give him another call if she needed to.

"So, my mom will visit and that's cool," Morgan told the horse. "The only problem is, I know she's gonna to ask me to go home to Chicago with her."

Bright Star stopped eating, raised her head and watched Morgan from the far corner of the stall.

Morgan breathed in the sweet smell of hay. She watched dust dance in the low sun's rays and she knew she was more at peace here than she'd ever been in her life before. "I'll tell her no," she said. "I don't want to go back to the city, at least not until your leg is healed and I've had time to work with you on the ranch."

Bright Star rustled across the straw to Morgan. Her head reached out and she nuzzled Morgan's knee.

Morgan leaned forward to stroke her. "You like it here at Three Horseshoes, don't you?" she whispered. "You and me both."

Bright Star gazed into Morgan's eyes.

"So I reckon I'll stay a while," Morgan said. "One day I'll have to go home with my mom. But till then, I'll stay and take care of you."

And she put her arms around Bright Star's neck and hugged her tight.

Our books are tested
for children and young people by
children and young people.

Thanks to everyone who consulted on
a manuscript for their time and effort in
helping us to make our books better
for our readers.